Jack and The Beanstalk

Illustrated by Pam Storey

Story re-told by Grace De La Touche

©1993 Grandreams Limited.

Published by
Grandreams Limited
Jadwin House, 205/211 Kentish Town Road, London, NW5 2JU.

Printed in Italy.   GS1-4

Long ago, in a land far away, a poor woman and her only son Jack lived in a tumbledown house. One day the woman found that they had no food and no money to buy any more.

"Jack!" called the woman.

"Yes, mother," said Jack, who was beginning to feel hungry.

"Jack, you must take the cow to market and sell her," said his mother. "Make sure that you get a good price for her, as she's all we have left and we need the money to buy food."

Jack went to the field and tied a rope around the cow's neck. The cow followed along behind Jack as he walked down the road towards the town.

Suddenly he was not alone. There was a small old man walking beside him. Jack was very surprised. Where had the man come from?

"That's a nice cow," said the strange man.

"Yes, she is," said Jack. "But she won't be ours for much longer."

"Why's that?" asked the old man.

"I'm off to market to sell her," said Jack.

"I'll buy her," said the old man.

"I must go to the market," said Jack. "I must get the best price I can."

"I'll give you a good price for her," said the man.

"How much?" asked Jack.

"Seven magic beans," said the man, and he held up a pouch.

"Beans!" exclaimed Jack.

"Magic beans," said the man. "I'll give you the beans for the cow, and life will be different for you."

"It certainly will be different," said Jack. "My mother would not be very happy if I came home with a handful of beans. I'm sorry, but I must sell her at the market."

"You will not be very successful," said the man. "But go if you must. I'll see you later. Goodbye."

"Goodbye," said Jack, and he carried on into town.

The market was very busy, and Jack stood in the middle, calling out that his cow was for sale. But nobody spoke to him, or even looked at the cow.

"I'm asking a good price," he called.

But no-one bought the cow. At the end of the afternoon everyone started packing up.

Jack still had his cow.

"Come on," he said to the cow. "I'll have to take you home." As he walked, the strange little man appeared again.

"You still have your cow," he said to Jack. "I still have the seven magic beans."

Jack stopped and thought. 'If I go home with the cow, we'll have nothing to eat. But if the beans are magic, then maybe things will change.'

"Very well," he said. "I'll take the beans."

"A wise choice," said the old man. "Good luck, and goodbye."

"Thank you for the beans," said Jack, and he headed for home. He looked back once, but the strange man was nowhere to be seen.

"Beans!" shouted his mother, when she saw what Jack had been given for the cow. "How will beans feed us?"

"They're magic beans," said Jack.

"Magic! How stupid!" said his mother. "Oh you silly boy!" And she threw the beans out of the window.

They both went to bed hungry.

When Jack woke the next morning, the light through his window was green.

"How strange," said Jack, and he went to the window. A strange sight met his eyes. A huge green trunk was growing past his window, with enormous leaves, blocking out the light.

"Jack!" called his mother.
"What is it?"

Jack ran downstairs and
looked outside.

"It's the beans!" he said.
"It's growing just where you
threw the beans last night.
Look how high it is."

They both looked up and
the beanstalk seemed to be
growing right up into the sky,
disappearing into the clouds.

"I'm going to climb it," said Jack suddenly.

"Oh, Jack," said his mother. "Is that a good idea? You don't know where it goes."

"I'll find out," said Jack. He went to the base of the beanstalk and began climbing.

"That man said life would be different," Jack called, and he climbed up and up.

Jack climbed so high that he went through the damp, white clouds. On the other side, the beanstalk finished. A path stretched away in front of Jack. In the distance he could see a castle.

When he reached the castle, he stood before the enormous gate and pulled on the bell.

A large woman came to the door.

"How did you get here?" she asked. "Come in, before my husband arrives home."

Jack was taken into the kitchen. Everything seemed to be enormous. The table and chair were like mountains to him.

"You must be hungry," said the woman. "Have some breakfast."

Jack was given a plate of food and he tucked into it as the climb had made him very hungry.

Loud footsteps could suddenly be heard.

"That's my husband," said the woman. "You must hide. He will eat a small boy like you."

Jack hid behind the oven door, but watched to see who came in.

"FEE, FO, FI, FUM, I smell the blood of an English man. Be he alive or be he dead, I'll grind his bones to make my bread!" shouted the giant as he come in to the kitchen.

"You're imagining things," said his wife.
"There's no Englishman here. Your breakfast is
on the table."

Jack watched as the giant sat and ate his
breakfast. Every so often he stopped and
sniffed. He muttered and then carried on
eating.

Finally, when he was full, he called out to
his wife.

"Bring me my golden hen," he said.

The hen was tiny, and sat on the table in front of the giant.

"Lay, golden hen," said the giant. The hen began to lay eggs, but they were golden eggs.

Jack looked at this from his hiding place.

'My mother would like a hen like that,' he thought, and he watched and waited.

The giant was full from his breakfast, and
he soon began to snore. Soon he was fast asleep.

This was Jack's chance. He jumped up
and climbed on to the table. He crept past the
giant, and picked up the hen and then ran. He
ran as fast as he could, out of the castle, along
the path, and then down the beanstalk.

His mother was very relieved to see him,
and she was delighted with the hen that laid
golden eggs. They would never go hungry again.

Jack began to get bored after a while. All their money problems were solved and they now had plenty to eat and new clothes to wear.

One day, he said to his mother, "I'm going to climb the beanstalk again."

"But why?" she asked. "We have all we need."

"I want to see what else is up there," said Jack, and he again climbed the beanstalk.

This time when he reached the castle, he

crept in and hid in a drawer.

After a while, he heard the loud footsteps.

"FEE, FO, FI, FUM, I smell the blood of an Englishman. Be he alive or be he dead, I'll grind his bones to make my bread," boomed the giant. "This time I'll find him."

"I'll help you," said his wife. "The naughty boy took your favourite hen."

The giant and his wife looked high and low, but they did not find Jack.

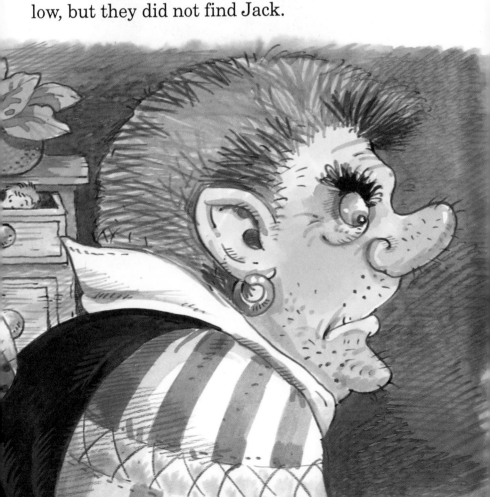

"Don't upset yourself anymore, my dear," said the giant's wife. "Eat your dinner, and then have a rest."

The giant sat down and began to eat. Jack was in the drawer right underneath his nose. The giant sniffed every so often.

When he had finished, he called to his wife.

"Bring me my harp," he said. "It can sing me to sleep."

His wife brought the harp and put it on the table in front of him. The giant stroked the strings and the harp began to sing by itself. The giant smiled, and yawned.

The harp sang and sang, and soon the giant was snoring.

Jack thought the harp was the most beautiful thing he had ever seen.

As soon as the giant was fast asleep, he jumped out of the drawer and grabbed the harp.

"Master! Master!" shouted the harp, "Help me!"

Jack had to run faster than ever before. The giant leapt up from his chair, shouting "FEE, FO, FI, FUM!" He ran after Jack, out through the door and along the path.

Jack ran as fast as he could, and when he came to the beanstalk, he climbed down as fast as he could. The beanstalk began to shake as the roaring giant climbed down after him.

"Mother!" called Jack, as soon as he could see the cottage beneath him. "Mother, bring me an axe!"

His mother took one look up the beanstalk and ran to fetch an axe.

When Jack was on the ground, his mother took the harp and handed him the axe.

WHACK! WHACK! went the axe, cutting into the beanstalk.

"Faster!" cried his mother.

"FEE, FO, FI, FUM!" bellowed the giant.

WHACK! the axe cut through the beanstalk and suddenly the whole thing began to fall over.

Over it went, taking the giant with it.

CRASH! The beanstalk landed, making a huge hole and the giant tumbled down the hole, never to be seen again.

Jack and his mother lived happily ever after, and with the golden hen they never had to worry about money again and Jack had the harp to sing him off to sleep every night.